Friendship Triumphs Over Cheat

By Joy E. Quiamco

ISBN
Hardbound-978-621-495-282-3
Softbound/Paperback-978-621-495-283-0
Mobile/ Kindle-978-621-495-284-7

Published by:
Poetry Planet Book Publishing House
Rosario, Pozorrubio, Pangasinan, Philippines
Contact Number:075-6155455
Email: maritesritumalta@gmail.com

PREFACE

The story "Friendship Triumphs Over Cheat" revolves around the friendship of two students, Sarah and Sam, who have been close friends since grade school. Despite their strong bond, an incident tests the strength of their friendship. Sarah catches Sam cheating during a test, which leaves her feeling conflicted and disappointed. She confides in her cousin, Pheb, who advises her to talk to Sam and encourage her to acknowledge her actions.

Eventually, Sarah confronts Sam, who is initially defensive but soon feels ashamed and apologizes for her mistake. Sarah, wanting to help her make things right, encourages her to admit the cheating to their teacher. Together, they approach Mrs. Cloribel, their teacher, to confess. Although disappointed, she appreciates their honesty and gives Sam a chance to make amends.

The story highlights themes of honesty, accountability, and the strength of true friendship in overcoming challenges.

ABC HIGH SC

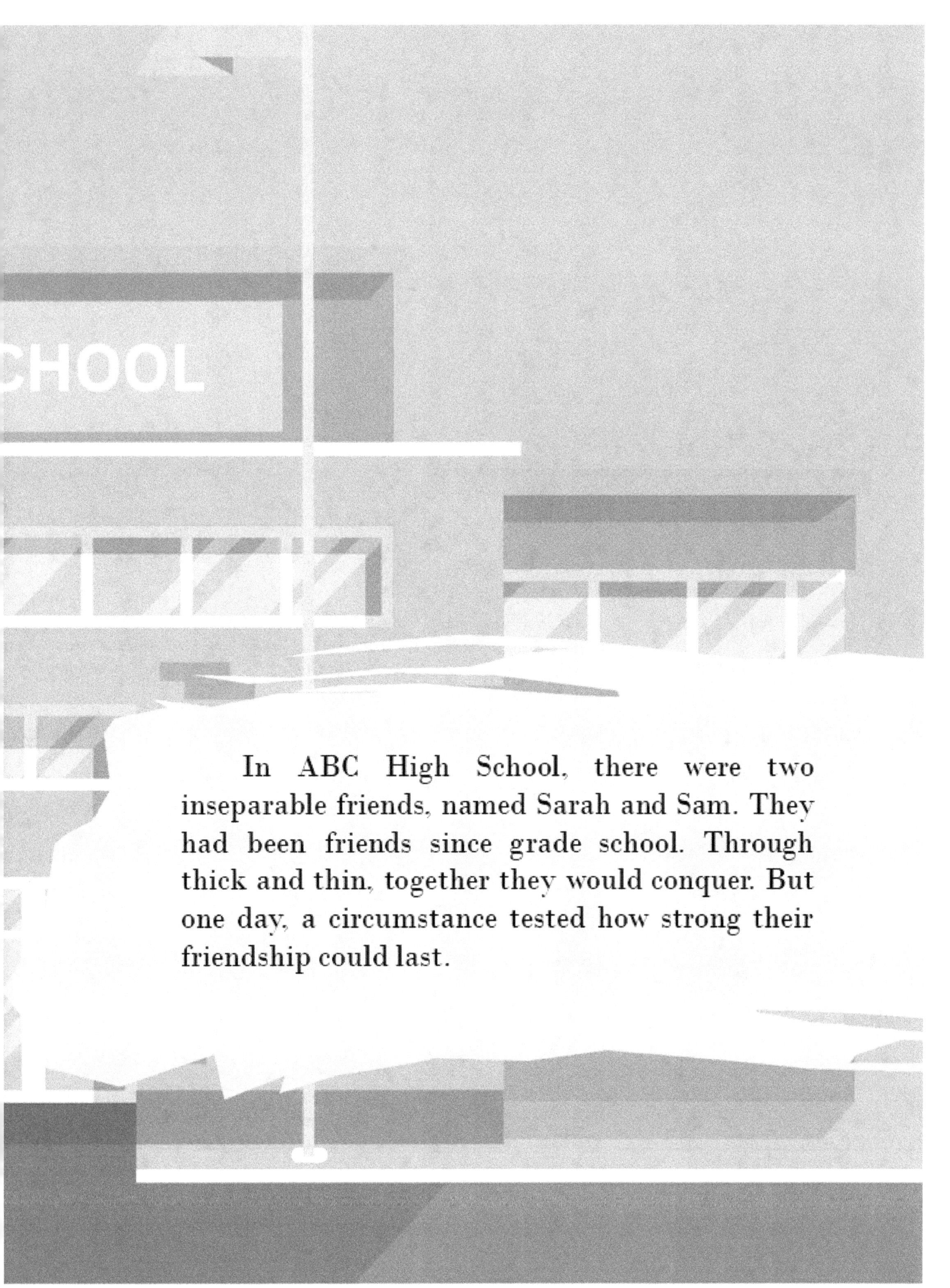

In ABC High School, there were two inseparable friends, named Sarah and Sam. They had been friends since grade school. Through thick and thin, together they would conquer. But one day, a circumstance tested how strong their friendship could last.

On that day, before their quiz, Sarah and Sam went to the library, diligently studying.

On the quiz day, Sam was sneaking answers on her phone. Sarah was shocked and confused, for they had studied. "It just didn't make sense," Sarah thought to herself.

After the exam, Sam quickly went home while Sarah went with her cousin. They ate and sat in the school cafeteria during lunchtime. Sarah seems sad at that moment.

Pheb asked, "Is everything okay?"

Sarah replied, "No, not really. I had a bad day today. I caught Sam cheating in Mrs. Cloribel's class."

Pheb, "What? Sam is cheating? Are you sure about that?"

Sarah sadly said, "Yes, we're always sitting beside each other, and then she sneaks at her phone scrolling looking for answers."

Pheb was shocked and replied, "Seriously? That's something I never thought she'd do. Sam's always been so against doing bad things, especially cheating."

Sarah replied, "I thought the same thing. What am I supposed to do? She's my best friend. Why do I feel like I'm in a tough spot?"

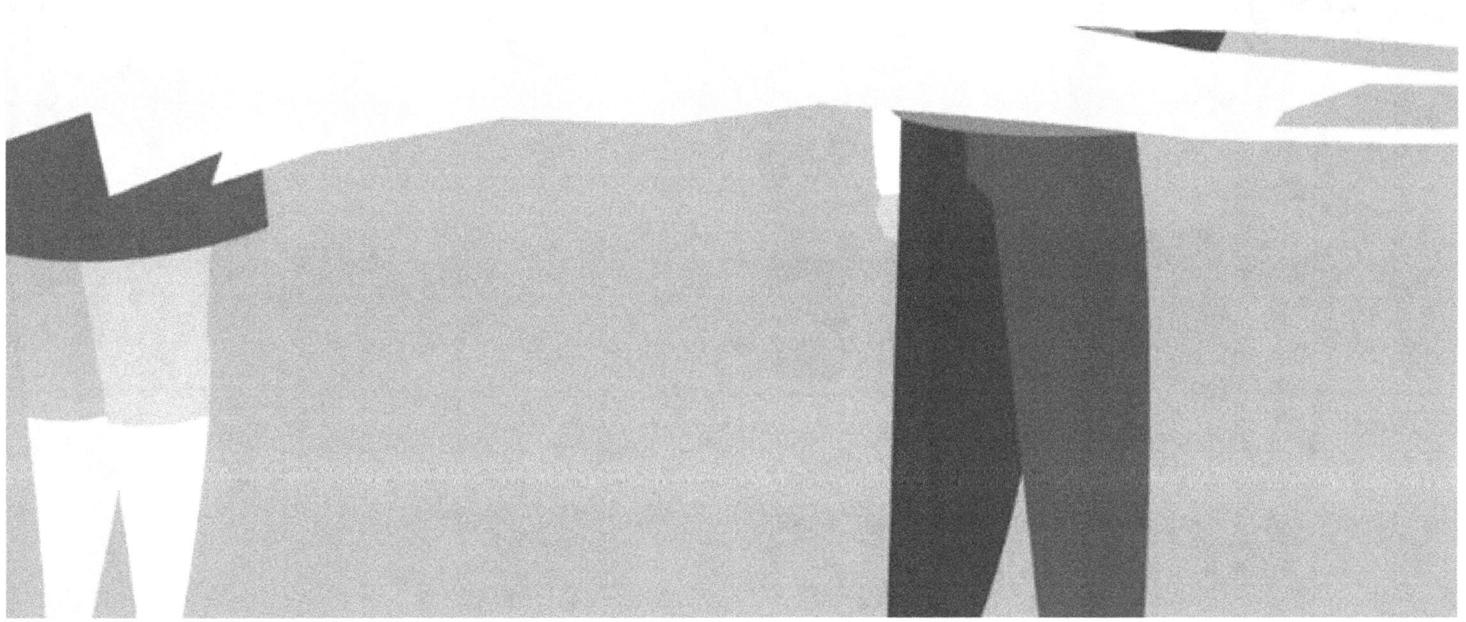

"Talk with her. She needs to know that cheating won't helpher move to the top. Tell her right away before it turns into a habit," Pheb suggested.

"I'm scared. What if that ends our friendship? I don't want to break her trust," Sarah said in a shaking voice.

Pheb said, "You've been her best friend for a long time, I'm sure she'll get it. Make her understand the consequences of her actions," Pheb said.

"Yeah, you're right. Sometimes, people need someone to wake them up from wrongdoings. Anyway, thanks for comforting me and giving me some advice, Pheb," Sarah said.

Sam replied, "I know, Sarah. I screwed up. I'm sorry. I was just so scared of failing the quiz, and I thought I could get away with it." When Sam heard her friend's statement, it hurt her.

"Sam, I'm disappointed in you," Sarah said firmly. "But I'm your best friend and also want to help you. Let's talk to Mrs. Cloribel and come clean about what happened."

Sam thought about what might be the consequences afterward, her mind was filled with fear, and she paused for a moment. Despite this, she knew Sarah was right. She breathed deeply, nodded, and went to the office, where she admitted she had done wrong.

Sam replied, "I know, Sarah. I screwed up. I'm sorry. I was just so scared of failing the quiz, and I thought I could get away with it." When Sam heard her friend's statement, it hurt her.

"Sam, I'm disappointed in you," Sarah said firmly. "But I'm your best friend and also want to help you. Let's talk to Mrs. Cloribel and come clean about what happened."

Sam thought about what might be the consequences afterward, her mind was filled with fear, and she paused for a moment. Despite this, she knew Sarah was right. She breathed deeply, nodded, and went to the office, where she admitted she had done wrong.

Together, they went to their teacher and confessed to what had happened during the quiz. Mrs. Cloribel was disappointed, yet admired their courage and integrity in admitting a mistake.

Their teacher appreciated their honesty and gave her a chance to make things right. For she doesn't let time pass by and tell what she had done wrong. Sam felt embarrassed and happy because there's no guilt anymore that he/ she carries.

Sam nodded and said, "I see now that cheating never pays off in the end. From now on, I will focus on being honest and studying my best." Sam promised herself she would never cheat again.

Sam vowed to never cheat again and commit to speaking the truth, knowing that true success could only be achieved through resilience and perseverance. From that day forward, Sarah and Sam's friendship became stronger, and they learned about honesty and integrity.

From that day on, through all of high school's ups and downs, they came out stronger than ever.

Genuine friends support one another and cooperate to avoid destroying the bond that has been formed. One can peace of mind by accepting one another's errors. Having a friend who is open to advice and accepting of mistakes is crucial.

ABOUT THE AUTHOR

Joy Estores-Quiamco, the author, is a secondary teacher from Dumingag, Zamboanga del Sur. Born on October 18, 1984, she graduated with a Bachelor of Secondary Education, majoring in English, and holds a Master of Arts in Education, specializing in English, from Saint Columban College, Pagadian City.

She has a natural talent for writing various forms of literature, such as poetry, essays, and stories. In fact, she is an active coach for young student writers in the field of Campus Journalism.

Publishing this book is a significant milestone for the author, as it is her first children's book. This work was created with the aim of providing educational content for children across the country. The inspiration for this book came from observing the dynamics of relationships around her, both in real life and in stories she has encountered. The experiences of friends who faced misunderstandings, moments of doubt, and even deceit led her to reflect on what makes friendships endure and triumph.

She is immensely grateful to her own friends, who have been her support and her inspiration, and to everyone who encouraged her to bring this story to life. Their companionship and faith have taught her the very lessons she hope to convey here—that genuine connections can weather any storm and that forgiveness often leads to unexpected strength.

As a secondary school English teacher with 17 years of experience, I've spent much of my career exploring the complexities of human relationships through literature, language, and real-life interactions. Teaching has given me a unique perspective on the power of friendship, trust, and resilience—qualities that inspired me to write this story, Friendship Triumphs Over Cheat.

Throughout my years as an educator and adviser, I have witnessed the strength and depth of friendships that students form, even as they navigate challenges and misunderstandings. These experiences have shown me that, while friendships can be tested by deceit or betrayal, true bonds can ultimately overcome these obstacles and emerge even stronger.

Outside of my professional life, I am a devoted parent, a supportive spouse, and a friend who values honesty and loyalty. My own friendships and family have shown me the importance of forgiveness and understanding, lessons that I hope to share through this story.

It brings me great joy to present Friendship Triumphs Over Cheat to readers. I hope it serves as a reminder that genuine friendship, rooted in trust and forgiveness, has the power to overcome any betrayal. Thank you for allowing me to be a part of your journey through this story.

JOY E. QUIAMCO
The Author

www.ingramcontent.com/pod-product-compliance
Lightning Source LLC
LaVergne TN
LVHW060832170826
845678LV00010B/1966

9786214952830